"It Moved!"

GEORGE   Kristina   Tariq

Roberta   DEREK   CANd

MARIA   Arif

Lily

SaRah   PETER

Books by the same author:

ANNE FINE

"It Moved!"

illustrations by
Katharine McEwen

**WALKER
BOOKS**

First published 2006 by Walker Books Ltd
87 Vauxhall Walk, London SE11 5HJ

2 4 6 8 10 9 7 5 3 1

Text © 2006 Anne Fine
Illustrations © 2006 Katharine McEwen

The right of Anne Fine and Katharine McEwen to be
identified as author and illustrator respectively of this work
has been asserted by them in accordance with the
Copyright, Designs and Patents Act 1988

This book has been typeset in Palatino

Printed and bound by Creative Print and Design (Wales), Ebbw Vale

British Library Cataloguing in Publication Data:
a catalogue record for this book is available from the British Library

ISBN-13: 978-1-4063-0013-0
ISBN-10: 1-4063-0013-6

www.walkerbooks.co.uk

For Isaac, Oliver and Rosa
A.F.

With lots of love to Emilia
K.M.

chapter one

Lily laid the big grey stone carefully on the teacher's desk and turned to the class.

"Is that what you've brought in to show us?" Mrs Bentley asked.

Lily nodded.

"But that's a stone," Arif was already saying.

"Just a lumpy old stone," agreed Maria.

The others were all joining in now.

"You can't just bring in some old stone for your turn at Show and Tell."

"We've all seen stones before, thanks."

Candy's soft eyes opened wide. "Lily," she whispered. "Is that the

 most interesting thing in your whole life? Some old stone?"

Lily looked around the class.
"No," she said.
"There are lots
of interesting
things in my life."
She thought about
the computer game
she'd been playing
only the day before.

But you
weren't allowed
to bring computer
games into school
any more – not since
Arif's went missing.

She thought about the
chocolate rabbit on her
dressing table. But if she'd
brought that in, she
would have felt
she ought
to offer
tiny bits of it round,

and there wouldn't have

been any left.

And she hadn't wanted to bring in
any of her string puppets because,
when Shaleema brought
in hers, the strings
had got tangled
so badly it
never came
right again.

So she

had brought

the stone.

13

There was a silence. Everyone stared.

Then Arif started complaining again. "But it's just an old stone."

"Not just any old stone," Lily argued.

"Yes, it is."

"No, it isn't. It's a nice lumpy shape, and a lovely rich grey colour, and it has weird little pockmarks on one side, and faint wavy lines along the other."

They were all criticizing now. "Just like every other stone in the whole wide world!"

"We have a hundred stones like that in our garden."

"So do we. Thousands!"

"Mrs Bentley! Mrs Bentley! Please tell us we didn't have to get out of bed and come all the way to school this morning just to look at an old stone!"

Mrs Bentley glanced anxiously at Lily.
"Well, dear," she said. "The class is right
in one way. It does look a little bit like
any old stone. So is there anything
special you'd like to tell us about it?"

Lily considered. There wasn't anything *particularly* special about the stone except that, of all the stones in their garden, it was her very favourite. It was big and heavy and grey, and sort of egg-shaped, apart from its rather flat bottom that meant it never, ever wobbled.

What could she tell them about it?

That her mother sometimes used it
to prop open the front gate?

Too boring.

That her father tripped over it every
single day when he came home
from work?

No. They might tease her about that afterwards.

Lily looked round the sea of faces staring back at her and took a deep breath.

"This stone is very special indeed," she told the class. "You see, it doesn't simply sit there like every other boring old stone in the world."

They carried on staring at her.

"Sometimes it moves."

chapter Two

At break-time, some people had to
stay behind to give lunch money
to Mrs Bentley. Each of them waited
their turn impatiently, then, one by one,
rushed out into the playground to join
the circle of people already sitting
around Lily's stone.

"Have we missed anything?"

"Has it moved yet?"

Kristina shook her head. "Tariq *thinks* it did," she said. "He says he was staring and staring and suddenly he thought he saw it move a little."

Tariq looked up from the stone. "I didn't say it *moved*, exactly," he corrected Kristina. "I said I thought it had a bit of a look of sort of *stretching* itself, that's all."

"*Stretching* itself?" said Peter.

"Yes," said Tariq.

"But stones don't *stretch* themselves," insisted Peter.

"They don't move, either," Sarah pointed out.

Everyone turned to glare at Sarah and Peter.

"Quick!" Lily said. "It's moving! Oh. Too late. You missed it."

Everyone stared at Lily suspiciously.

Then they went back to looking

at the stone.

"It hasn't moved very *far*," grumbled Arif. "It's almost exactly where it was before."

"*Almost* exactly?" scoffed Sarah. "It is *exactly* where it was before. It is a *stone*, and stones don't move unless you *move* them."

But they were ignoring her, all far more interested in listening to George demand of Lily, "*How* did it move?

Did it grow little legs?

Did it roll?

Did it heave itself over?

If you've seen it moving, Lily, tell us *how* it moves."

"I can't explain exactly," Lily defended herself. "It just sort of ... *does*."

As they all peered at her closely to
see if she was making it up, Roberta
startled them by saying, "It moved!
I saw it! I just saw it too!"

They turned to look at Roberta.
"Are you sure?"

Roberta went pink. "I'm sure. I *saw* it. Just then. It moved."

"You're not imagining it?"

Roberta went pinker. "No."

"You *might* have imagined it..."

Roberta's face was really red now. "I'm not an idiot," she snapped. "And I'm not a liar either. Are you calling me a liar?"

"No," Derek said hastily. "It just seems a little strange, that's all. I mean, here we are, watching the stone carefully for almost the whole of break-time, and nothing happens. We turn for just a few seconds to look at Sarah and Peter, and Lily sees the stone move. And then we turn the other way to look at Lily, and you say you saw it moving too."

"Tariq saw it as well," said Roberta.

"No," Tariq corrected. "I said I only *thought* I saw it moving. And not really moving, either. Just sort of *stretching*, if you know what I mean."

"No," Sarah said tartly, "I don't know what you mean."

Maria tried to make peace. "If the rest of us all spent a little more time watching the stone carefully instead of looking at Lily and Roberta and quarrelling with one another, then we might get to see it move too."

There was no arguing with that. So the rest of them settled back down again in their circle and stared at the big grey stone until the bell rang for the end of break.

chapter Three

When they spilled out again at lunchtime, the first ones to reach the playground were agreed.

"It's moved."

"It's definitely moved."

"Not much, but a little."

"Enough to prove it can."

"Somebody might have moved it," Peter offered.

Everyone turned on him. "Who?
Who's been out of class?
No one went
off to the
toilets...

No one was sent
along to Mrs Mackay's
office...

Nobody went

to the sickroom."

"It's true. Nobody left the classroom

the whole time we were there."

"It must have moved by itself."

"No other explanation."

"None."

Peter stared at his classmates. Then he took the cheese and tomato sandwich he hadn't wanted anyway out of his lunch box and laid it on the ground beside the stone.

"This isn't *any* old sandwich," he declared, glaring at Lily. "Oh no! This is a very *special* sandwich. You see, sometimes it *moves*."

"I don't believe you," said Kristina promptly.

"That's stupid," George said. "How can a sandwich move?"

"You're just jealous of Lily," said Candy.

"Listen," hissed Peter, close to losing his temper now. "A moving sandwich is *just* as likely as a moving stone."

"Not when you *think* about it," said Tariq.

"You can't be *thinking*," Peter almost shouted. "None of you can be *thinking*. If you were *thinking*, you would know that stones don't move."

Since they were sitting looking at him pityingly, he said it again even louder. "Stones don't move!"

"I think it just did again," said Roberta. "I think I just caught it moving out of the corner of my eye." She gave Peter a reproachful look. "And if you hadn't been shouting at us and distracting me, I would have seen it properly."

Peter clutched his head and doubled over. He looked like someone who'd been kicked in the stomach. He looked as if he were in terrible pain.

Sarah came to his rescue. She felt in her pockets and brought out the only thing she could find. It was a sweet wrapper. Sarah threw it on the ground, next to the sandwich.

"See this old sweet wrapper?" she said. "Well, that moves too. So why don't you all sit and watch it? That would be just as sensible as sitting around looking at a stone. You're just as likely to see it get up and move."

"I didn't say the stone actually *gets up* and moves," Lily tried to explain to them. "I just said it *moves*."

"And I only thought I saw it *stretching*," said Tariq.

"Stones–just–don't–move!" howled Peter.

"If you and Sarah don't think you're likely to see anything exciting," Maria told them soothingly, "you could go off and do something else till the bell rings, and we'll stay here to watch the stone."

"Good idea," Roberta muttered under her breath.

So Sarah and Peter went off in a huff

until nearly the end of the lunch break.

chapter Four

When Sarah and Peter came back,
everyone else was still in the circle.
The sweet wrapper had disappeared,
but the sandwich and stone were still
lying there.

"Well, well," said Peter. "Obviously the stone and the sandwich have been having such an interesting little chat that neither has bothered to move. But Sarah's sweet wrapper must have got really bored because it's gone off for a walk."

"Don't be silly," said Tariq.

"It was a *sweet* wrapper.

It just blew away."

"And that's a *stone*," said Peter. "It just *sits* there."

"As it happens," Kristina told him, "you're wrong about that. The stone has been moving quite a bit. Lots of people think they've seen it."

Peter's face went scarlet. He started dancing up and down, stamping his feet. His fists were clenched and there were tears  of frustration and rage in his eyes. He was in the most terrible temper.

"Shut *up*!" he shouted at Kristina. "Shut up and stop it! *All* of you! You're *mad*! You're *stupid*! Lily has put this daft idea in your heads and you've fallen for it. You have no sense at all. You're acting like *zombies*, sitting around in a circle watching a stone and waiting for it to move."

He jumped up and down on the spot
in his fury, shrieking at the top of his
voice. "How many times do I have to
tell you? STONES …

DON'T …

MOVE!"

One of the dinner ladies came over
and put an arm around Peter's shoulder.
"Now, now," she tried to soothe him.
"Calm down, my precious. There's
nothing in the world worth getting this
excited about."

Candy looked up at her. "Not even a stone that moves?"

The dinner lady looked at the circle of children sitting round watching the stone. Then she looked at the stone.

"Well," she said. "A stone that moves? That *would* be worth making a bit of a song and dance about. Why? Have you got one? Is that it?"

And she perched on the playground wall and kept her eye on the stone with the rest of them until the bell rang.

chapter five

It seemed like a very long afternoon. But gradually the hands on the classroom clock crawled round towards going-home time. Two minutes before the bell, Mrs Bentley wiped the last of the maths work off the board and asked the class as usual, "So what was the best bit of the day?"

Everyone's hand shot up.

Mrs Bentley asked Roberta first.

"Show and Tell," Roberta said. "Definitely!"

Almost everyone agreed. "Yes. Show and Tell!"

Mrs Bentley was somewhat startled. "You mean Lily's stone?"

"That's right."

"The big grey lumpy one?"

"Yes. That one. The one that moved."

"Well, that *is* a surprise," Mrs Bentley couldn't help saying. And then, in case she'd hurt Lily's feelings, she added, "Not that it wasn't a really interesting Show and Tell."

"I know," said Lily. "I knew you'd find it special."

Mrs Bentley looked around the class. No one was laughing. No one was even sniggering. Peter had his head in his hands, but he  could have been reading a book hidden on his lap. And Sarah was staring

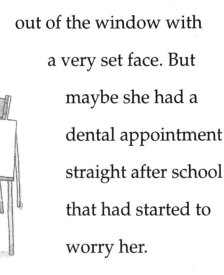

out of the window with a very set face. But maybe she had a dental appointment straight after school that had started to worry her.

In any case, Mrs Bentley couldn't

think of a thing to say. So she said what

she always did, but a minute or so

earlier than usual.

"Right, then. You can pack up your things now and leave the classroom. But quietly. Have a really good evening and see you tomorrow."

She went to the cupboard to check on the workbooks for the next morning, so she didn't notice everyone hanging about waiting for Lily to pack her bag, and then trailing her out to the playground.

When they got to the place where the stone lay, Maria said to Lily, "Are you taking it home now?"

"You bet," said Lily, and she scooped it up. "I'm not going to leave it here in case it gets kicked about."

"Or stolen."

"Or even runs away," Roberta said darkly.

"Like the sweet wrapper?" Peter asked nastily, but everyone ignored him.

Lily said cheerfully, "I don't think it would run away."

"You think it's happy, living with you?" asked Sarah sarcastically.

Lily ignored the sarcasm. "Happy enough," she said.

When Lily got home, her father asked her, "How was Show and Tell?"

"Not bad," said Lily.

"You finally decided what to talk to them about?"

"Yes," Lily told him. "I had a flash of inspiration at the last minute."

"Good," said her father. "I had an excellent day too. For the first time in as long as I can remember,

I didn't trip over that infernal stone when I came home from work."

"A good day all round, then," said Lily. "Except for poor Sarah and Peter."

"Why? What happened to them?" asked her father.

"Nothing," Lily said. "I'll tell you another time."

And she ran up the stairs to eat

a bit more of her chocolate rabbit,

and decide between playing with her

computer game or with one

of her string puppets.